Edward Rowland Sill

Hermione and Other Poems

Edward Rowland Sill

Hermione and Other Poems

ISBN/EAN: 9783744708081

Printed in Europe, USA, Canada, Australia, Japan

Cover: Foto ©Andreas Hilbeck / pixelio.de

More available books at **www.hansebooks.com**

HERMIONE

AND OTHER POEMS

BY

EDWARD ROWLAND SILL

BOSTON AND NEW YORK
HOUGHTON, MIFFLIN AND COMPANY
The Riverside Press, Cambridge
1899

NOTE

I N 1887 the publishers of this volume issued a small collection of Mr. Sill's poems under the title *Poems by Edward Rowland Sill.* In the prefatory note a brief account was given of the poet and his productions, and attention was drawn to the scattering of his poems during his lifetime in many forms of print and even with a variety of signatures. The volume then gathered was purposely small and gave a hint only of the activity of Mr. Sill's poetic nature.

Two years later a second collection was made, and published under the title *The Hermitage, and Later Poems,* with a tributary lyric by Mr. Aldrich. These two volumes have won many readers, and the strong personal interest in Mr. Sill thus created has led to an urgent demand for a still further collection of his scattered

poems.   After a lapse of ten years, there-
fore, the publishers present a third and
final volume, in which they have endeav-
ored to gather from print and manuscript
such verses as may satisfy a demand created by reading an author who gave freely,
but after all would have set light store
upon many of his gifts.   Thus the three
volumes really contain a selection rather
than a collection of Mr. Sill's poetical
writings.

March, 1899.

CONTENTS

vi *Contents*

Contents

Dear artist of the storied land !
 I too have loved a heart of stone.
What was thy charm of voice or hand,
 Thy secret spell, Pygmalion ?

II

INFLUENCES

IF quiet autumn mornings would not come,
With golden light, and haze, and harvest
  wain,
And spices of the dead leaves at my feet ;
If sunsets would not burn through cloud,
  and stain
With fading rosy flush the dusky dome ;
If the young mother would not croon that
  sweet
Old sleep-song, like the robin's in the rain ;
If the great cloud-ships would not float
  and drift
Across such blue all the calm afternoon ;
If night were not so hushed ; or if the
  moon
Might pause forever by that pearly rift,

Nor fill the garden with its flood again ;
If the world were not what it still must be,
Then might I live forgetting love and
　　thee.

III

THE DEAD LETTER

THE letter came at last.　I carried it
To the deep woods unopened.　All the
　　trees
Were hushed, as if they waited what was
　　writ,
And feared for me.　Silent they let me sit
Among them ; leaning breathless while I
　　read,
And bending down above me where they
　　stood.
A long way off I heard the delicate tread
Of the light-footed loiterer, the breeze,
Come walking toward me in the leafy
　　wood.
I burned the page that brought me love
　　and woe.

At first it writhed to feel the spires of
  flame,
Then lay quite still; and o'er each word
  there came
Its white ghost of the ash, and burning
  slow
Each said: "You cannot kill the spirit;
  know
That we shall haunt you, even till heart
  and brain
Lie as we lie in ashes — all in vain."

IV

THE SONG IN THE NIGHT

In the deep night a little bird
  Wakens, or dreams he is awake:
Cheerily clear one phrase is heard,
  And you almost feel the morning break.

In the deep dark of loss and wrong,
  One face like a lovely dawn will thrill,
And all night long at my heart a song
  Suddenly stirs and then is still.

REPROOF IN LOVE

ECAUSE we are shut out from
    light,
    Each of the other's look and
    smile ;
Because the arms' and lips' delight
    Are past and dead, a weary while ;

Because the dawn, that joy has brought,
    Brings now but certainty of pain,
Nothing for you and me has bought
    The right to live our lives in vain.

Take not away the only lure
    That leads me on my lonely way,
To know you noble, sweet, and pure,
    Great in least service, day by day.

ES, I know what you say:
    Since it cannot be soul to soul,
Be it flesh to flesh, as it may;
    But is Earth the whole?

Shall a man betray the Past
    For all Earth gives?
"But the Past is dead?"   At last,
    It is all that lives.

Which were the nobler goal —
    To snatch at the moment's bliss,
Or to swear I will keep my soul
    Clean for her kiss?

6

ALONE

STILL earth turns and pulses stir,
   And each day hath its deed ;
But if I be dead to her,
   What is the life I lead ?

Cares the cuckoo for the wood,
   When the red leaves are down ?
Stays the robin near the brood,
   When they are fledged and flown ?

Yea, we live ; the common air
   To both its bounty brings.
Mockery !   Can the absent share
   The half-forgotten things ?

Barren comfort fancy doles
   To him that truly sees ;
Sullen Earth can sever souls,
   Far as the Pleiades.

Take thy toys, step-mother Earth, —
   Take force of limb and brain ;
All thy gifts are little worth,
   Till her I find again.

Grass may spring and buds may stir, —
   Why should mine eyes take heed ?
For if I be dead to her,
   Then am I dead indeed.

TO A MAID DEMURE

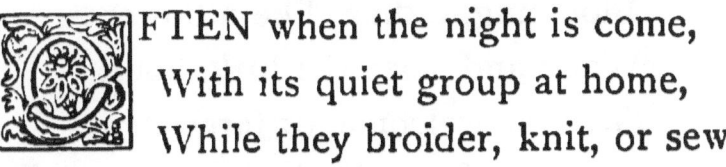FTEN when the night is come,
With its quiet group at home,
While they broider, knit, or sew,
Read, or chat in voices low,
Suddenly you lift your eyes
With an earnest look, and wise ;
But I cannot read their lore, —
Tell me less, or tell me more.

Like a picture in a book,
Pure and peaceful is your look,
Quietly you walk your ways ;
Steadfast duty fills the days.
Neither tears nor fierce delights,
Feverish days nor tossing nights,
Any troublous dreams confess, —
Tell me more, or tell me less.

Swift the weeks are on the wing ;
Years are brief, and love a thing

Blooming, fading, like a flower;
Wake and seize the little hour.
Give me welcome, or farewell;
Quick!   I wait!   And who can tell
What to-morrow may befall, —
Love me more, or not at all.

F I were very sure
    That all was over betwixt you
      and me —
That, while this endless absence I en-
    dure
With but one mood, one dream, one mis-
    ery
Of waiting, you were happier to be free, —

    Then I might find again
In cloud and stream and all the winds
    that blow,
    Yea, even in the faces of my fellow-
    men,
The old companionship ; and I might know
Once more the pulse of action, ere I go.

    But now I cannot rest,
While this one pleading, querulous tone
    without

Breaks in and mars the music in my
    breast.
I open the closed door — lo ! all about,
What seem your lingering footprints ; then
    I doubt.

Waken me from this sleep !
Strike fearless, let the naked truth-edge
    gleam !
For while the beautiful old past I keep,
I am a phantom, and all mortals seem
But phantoms, and my life fades as a
    dream.

THE WORLD RUNS ROUND [1]

THE world runs round,
  And the world runs well ;
  And at heaven's bound,
Weaving what the hours shall tell
Of the future way,
Sit the great Norns, sisters gray.
Now a thread of doom and hate,
Now a skein of life and love, —
Whether hearing shriek or psalm,
Hearts that curse or pray,
Most composed and very calm
Is their weaving, soon and late.

One man's noisy years go by,
Rich to the crowd's shallow eye,
Full of big and empty sound,

[1] For the Anniversary of the Overland Magazine, San Francisco, 1884.

Brandished gesture, voice profound,
Blustering benevolence,
Thin in deeds, and poor in pence.
Out of it all, so loud and long,
What one thread that 's clean and strong
To weave the coming good,
Can the great Norns find ?
But where some poor child stood,
And shrank, and wept its faultiness,
Out of that little life so blind
The great web takes a golden strand
That shall shine and that shall stand
The whole wide world to bless.

One man walks in silk :
Honey and milk
Flow thro' his days.
Corn loads his wains,
He hath all men's praise,
He sees his heart's desire.
In all his veins
What can the sorrowful Norns
Find of heroic fire ?

Another finds his ways
All blocked and barred.
Lonely, he grapples hard,
Sets teeth and bleeds.
Then the glad Norns
Know he succeeds,
With victory wrought
Greater than that he sought.

When will the world believe
Force is for him that is met and fought:
Storm hath no song till the pine resists;
Lightning no flame when it runs as it lists;
So do the wise Norns weave.
The world runs round,
And the world runs well:
It needs no prophet, when evil is found,
Good to foretell.

Many the voices
Ruffling the air:
This one rejoices,
That in despair

Past the sky-bars
Climbs to the stars.

One voice is heard
By the ocean's shore,
Speaking a word
Quiet and sane,
Amid the human rush and roar
Like a robin's song in the rain.
The red gold of the sun
Seems to stream in power
Already from behind the shower
When that song's begun.

It doth not insist, or claim ;
You may hear, or go :
It clamors not for gain or fame,
Tranquilly and slow
It speaketh unafraid,
Calls the spade, spade,
With the large sense mature
Of him that hath both sat, and roved,
And with a solemn undercurrent pure,
As his that now hath lived and loved.

Brightened with glimpse and gleam
Of mother-wit —
There is more salt in it,
More germ and sperm
Of the great things to be,
Than louder notes men speak and sing.

It is a voice of Spring,
Clear and firm.
Tones prophetic in it flow,
Steady and strong,
Yet soft and low —
An excellent thing in song.
" I can wait," saith merry Spring,
If the rain runneth, and the wind hum-
　　meth,
And the mount at morn be hoar with
　　snow,
In the frost the violet dozes,
Wind and rain bear breath of roses,
And the great summer cometh
Wherein all things shall gayly bloom and
　　grow.

Long may the voice be found,
Potent its spell,
While the world runs round,
And the world runs well.

RUEL and wild the battle:
Great horses plunged and reared,
And through dust - cloud and
smoke-cloud,
Blood-red with sunset's angry flush,
You heard the gun-shots rattle,
And, 'mid hoof-tramp and rush,
The shrieks of women speared.

For it was Russ and Turkoman, —
No quarter asked or given ;
A whirl of frenzied hate and death
Across the desert driven.
Look ! the half-naked horde gives way,
Fleeing frantic without breath,
Or hope, or will ; and on behind
The troopers storm, in blood-thirst blind,
While, like a dreadful fountain-play,

The swords flash up, and fall, and slay —
Wives, grandsires, baby brows and gray,
Groan after groan, yell upon yell —
Are men but fiends, and is earth hell?

Nay, for out of the flight and fear
Spurs a Russian cuirassier;
In his arms a child he bears.
Her little foot bleeds; stern she stares
Back at the ruin of her race.
The small hurt creature sheds no tear,
Nor utters cry; but clinging still
To this one arm that does not kill,
She stares back with her baby face.

Apart, fenced round with ruined gear,
The hurrying horseman finds a space,
Where, with face crouched upon her knee,
A woman cowers.   You see him stoop
And reach the child down tenderly,
Then dash away to join his troop.

How came one pulse of pity there —
One heart that would not slay, but save —

In all that Christ-forgotten sight?
Was there, far north by Neva's wave,
Some Russian girl in sleep-robes white,
Making her peaceful evening prayer,
That Heaven's great mercy 'neath its care
Would keep and cover him to-night?

NE, or a thousand voices? — fill-
ing noon
With such an undersong and
drowsy chant
As sings in ears that waken from a swoon,
And know not yet which world such
murmurs haunt:
Single, then double beats, reiterant;
Far off and near; one ceaseless, change-
less tune.

If bird or breeze awake the dreamy will
We lose the song, as it had never been;
Then suddenly we find 't is singing still
And had not ceased. So, friend of
mine, within
My thoughts one underthought, beneath
the din
Of life, doth every quiet moment fill.

Thy voice is far, thy face is hid from me,
But day and night are full of dreams of
    thee.

NOT a dread cavern, hoar with
damp and mould,
Where I must creep, and in the
dark and cold,
Offer some awful incense at a shrine
That hath no more divine
Than that 't is far from life, and stern,
and old;

But a bright hill-top in the breezy air,
Full of the morning freshness high and
clear,
Where I may climb and drink the pure,
new day,
And see where winds away
The path that God would send me, shin-
ing fair.

ON SECOND THOUGHT

THE end 's so near,
 It is all one
What track I steer,
 What work 's begun.
 It is all one
 If *nothing* 's done,
The end 's so near !

The end 's so near,
 It is all one
What track thou steer,
 What work 's begun —
 Some deed, *some* plan,
 As thou 'rt a man !
The end 's so near !

HIS LOST DAY

ROWING old, and looking back
  Wistfully along his track,
  I have heard him try to tell,
With a smile a little grim,
Why a world he loved so well
Had no larger fruit of him: —

'T was one summer, when the time
Loiterëd like drowsy rhyme,
Sauntering on his idle way
Somehow he had lost a day.
Whether 't was the daisies meek,
Keeping Sabbath all the week,
Birds without one work-day even,
Or the little pagan bees,
Busy all the sunny seven, —
Whether sleep at afternoon,
Or much rising with the moon,
Couching with the morning star,

Or enchantments like to these,
Had confused his calendar, —

"It is Saturday," men said.
"Nay, 't is Friday," obstinate
Clung the notion in his head.
Had the cloudy sisters three
In their weaving of his fate,
Dozed, and dropped a stitch astray?

"'T was the losing of that day
Cost my fortune," he would say.
"On that day I should have writ
Screeds of wisdom and of wit;
Should have sung the missing song,
Wonderful, and sweet, and strong;
Might have solved men's doubt and dream
With some waiting truth supreme.
If another thing there be
That a groping hand may miss
In a twilight world like this,
Those lost hours its grace and glee
Surely would have brought to me."

FERTILITY

LEAR water on smooth rock
     Could give no foot-hold for a
          single flower,
Or slenderest shaft of grain:
The stone must crumble under storm and
     rain —
The forests crash beneath the whirlwind's
     power —
And broken boughs from many a tempest-
     shock,
And fallen leaves of many a wintry hour,
Must mingle in the mould,
Before the harvest whitens on the plain,
Bearing an hundred-fold.
Patience, O weary heart!
Let all thy sparkling hours depart,
And all thy hopes be withered with the
     frost,
And every effort tempest-tost —

So, when all life's green leaves
Are fallen, and mouldered underneath the
      sod,
Thou shalt go not too lightly to thy God,
But heavy with full sheaves.

THE MYSTERY

NEVER know why 't is I love
thee so :
   I do not think 't is that thine
eyes for me
Grow bright as sudden sunshine on the
sea ;
Nor for thy rose-leaf lips, or breast of
snow,
Or voice like quiet waters where they flow.

So why I love thee well I cannot tell :
   Only it is that when thou speak'st to me
   'T is thy voice speaks, and when thy
face I see
It is thy face I see ; and it befell
Thou wert, and I was, and I love thee
well.

THE LOST BIRD

HAT cared she for the free
    hearts ? She would comfort
      The prisoned one :
What recked I of the wanton other sing-
    ers ?
    She sang for me alone —
    Was all my own, my own !

But when they loaded me with heavier
    fetters,
    And chained I lay,
How could she know I longed to reach
    her window ?
    Athirst the livelong day,
    At eve she fled away.

Still stands her cage wide open at the
    casement,
    In sun and rain,

31

Though years have gone, and rust has
    thickly gathered, —
        My watching all in vain ;
        She will not come again.

Against its wires 1 strum with idle fin-
    gers
        From morn to noon ;
I swing the door with loitering touch,
    and listen
        To hear that old-time tune,
        Sweet as the soul of June.

My bird, my silver voice that cheered
    my prison,
        Hushed, lost to me:
And still I wait for death, in chains, for-
    saken,
        (Soon may the summons be !)
        But she is free.

                    — " Is free ? "

Nay, in the palace porches caught and
    hanging,

Who says 't is gay —
The song the false prince hears? who
    says her singing,
    From day to summer day,
    Grieves not her heart away?

But when my dream comes true in that
    last sleeping,
    And death makes free,
Against the blue shall snowy wings come
    sweeping,
    My bird flown back to me,
    Mine for eternity!

E true to me! For there will
  dawn a day
When thou wilt find the faith
  that now I see,
Bow at the shrines where I must bend
  the knee,
Knowing the great from small.   Then
  lest thou say,
"Ah me, that I had never flung away
His love who would have stood so close
  to me
Where now I walk alone " — lest there
  should be
Such vain regret, Love, oh be true !   But
  nay,
Not true to me: true to thine own high
  quest
Of truth ; the aspiration in thy breast,
Noble and blind, that pushes by my hand,

And will not lean, yet cannot surely
    stand ;
True to thine own pure heart, as mine to
    thee
Beats true. So shalt thou best be true
    to me.

SUMMER AFTERNOON

AR in hollow mountain cañons
Brood with purple-folded pinions,
Flocks of drowsy distance-colors
on their nests;
And the bare round slopes for forests
Have cloud-shadows, floating forests,
On their breasts.

Winds are wakening and dying,
Questions low with low replying,
Through the oak a hushed and trem-
bling whisper goes:
Faint and rich the air with odors,
Hyacinth and spicy odors
Of the rose.

Even the flowerless acacia
Is one flower — such slender stature,
With its latticed leaves a-tremble in the
sun:

They have shower-drops for blossoms,
Quivering globes of diamond-blossoms,
    Every one.

In the blue of heaven holy
Clouds go floating, floating slowly,
Pure in snowy robe and sunny silver
    crown ;
And they seem like gentle angels —
Leisure-full and loitering angels,
    Looking down.

Half the birds are wild with singing,
And the rest with rhythmic winging
Sing in melody of motion to the sight ;
    Every little sparrow twitters,
    Cheerily chirps, and cheeps, and twit-
    ters
    His delight.

Sad at heart amid the splendor,
Dull to all the radiance tender,
What can I for such a world give back
    again ?

Could I only hint the beauty —
Some least shadow of the beauty,
Unto men !

ROM the warm garden in the
    summer night
  All faintest odors came : the tube-
    rose white
Glimmered in its dark bed, and many a
    bloom
Invisibly breathed spices on the gloom.
It stirred a trouble in the man's dull
    heart,
A vexing, mute unrest : " Now what thou
    art,
Tell me ! " he said in anger.   Something
    sighed,
" I am the poor ghost of a ghost that died
In years gone by."   And he recalled of
    old
A passion dead — long dead, even then —
    that came
And haunted many a night like this, the
    same

In their dim hush above the fragrant
    mould
And glimmering flowers, and troubled all
    his breast.
" Rest ! " then he cried ; " perturbëd spirit,
    rest ! "

A THUNDER – STORM of the olden days!
The red sun sinks in a sleepy haze;
The sultry twilight, close and still,
Muffles the cricket's drowsy trill.
Then a round-topped cloud rolls up the west,
Black to its smouldering, ashy crest,
And the chariot of the storm you hear,
With its jarring axle rumbling near;
Till the blue is hid, and here and there
The sudden, blinding lightnings glare.
Scattering now the big drops fall,
Till the rushing rain in a silver wall
Blurs the line of the bending elms,
Then blots them out and the landscape whelms.
A flash — a clap, and a rumbling peal:
The broken clouds the blue reveal;

The last bright drops fall far away,
And the wind, that had slept for heat all
　　　day,
With a long-drawn sigh awakes again
And drinks the cool of the blessed rain.

November ! night, and a sleety storm :
Close are the ruddy curtains, warm
And rich in the glow of the roaring grate.
It may howl outside like a baffled fate,
And rage on the roof, and lash the pane
With its fierce and impotent wrath in
　　　vain.
Sitting within at our royal ease
We sing to the chime of the ivory keys,
And feast our hearts from script and
　　　score
With the wealth of the mellow hearts of
　　　yore.

A winter's night on a world of snow !
Not a sound above, not a stir below :
The moon hangs white in the icy air,
And the shadows are motionless every-
　　　where.

Is this the planet that we know —
This silent floor of the ghostly snow?
Or is this the moon, so still and dead,
And yonder orb far overhead,
With its silver map of plain and sea,
Is that the earth where we used to be?
Shall we float away in the frosty blue
To that living, summer world we knew,
With its full, hot heart-beats as of old,
Or be frozen phantoms of the cold?

A river of ice, all blue and glare,
Under a star-shine dim and rare.
The sheeny sheet in the sparkling light
Is ribbed with slender wisps of white —
Crinkles of snow, that the flying steel
Lightly crunches with ringing heel.
Swinging swift as the swallows skim,
You round the shadowy river's rim :
Falling somewhere out of the sky
Hollow and weird is the owlet's cry;
The gloaming woods seem phantom hosts,
And the bushes cower in the snow like
        ghosts.

Till the tinkling feet that with you glide
Skate closer and closer to your side,
And something steals from a furry muff,
And you clasp it and cannot wonder
     enough
That a little palm so soft and fair
Could keep so warm in the frosty air.

'T is thus we dream in our tranquil clime,
Rooted still in the olden time ;
Longing for all those glooms and gleams
Of passionate Nature's mad extremes.
Or was it only our hearts, that swelled
With the youth and life and love they
     held ?

FULFILLMENT

ALL the skies had gloomed in gray,
  Many a week, day after day.
  Nothing came the blank to fill,
Nothing stirred the stagnant will.
Winds were raw ; buds would not swell :
Some malign and sullen spell
Soured the currents of the year,
And filled the heart with lurking fear.

In his room he moped and glowered,
Where the leaden daylight lowered ;
Drummed the casement, turned his book,
Hating nature's hostile look.

Suddenly there came a day
When he flung his gloom away.
Something hinted help was near :
Winds were fresh and sky was clear ;
Light he stepped, and firmly planned, —
Some good news was close at hand

Truly : for when day was done,
He was lying all alone,
Fretted pulse had ceased to beat,
Very still were hands and feet,
And the robins through the long
Twilight sang his slumber song.

THE SINGER

ILLY bird !
When his mate is near,
Not a note of singing shall you
hear.
Take his little love away,
Half the livelong day
Will his tune be heard —
Silly bird !

Sunny days
Silent basks he in the light,
Little sybarite !
But when all the room
Darkens in the gloom,
And the rain
Pours and pours along the pane,
He is bent
(Ah, the small inconsequent !)
On defying all the weather ;

Rain and cloud and storm together
Naught to him,
Singing like the seraphim.

So we know a poet's ways :
Sunny days,
Silent he
In his fine serenity ;
But if winds are loud,
He will pipe beneath the cloud ;
And if one is far away,
Sings his heart out, as to say, —
" It may be
She will hear and come to me."

THE THINGS THAT WILL NOT DIE

HAT am I glad will stay when I
    have passed
  From this dear valley of the
    world, and stand
On yon snow-glimmering peaks, and linger-
    ing cast
    From that dim land
  A backward look, and haply stretch my
    hand,
Regretful, now the wish comes true at
    last ?

Sweet strains of music I am glad will be
  Still wandering down the wind, for men
    will hear
And think themselves from all their care
    set free,
    And heaven near

When summer stars burn very still and
   clear,
And waves of sound are swelling like the
   sea.

And it is good to know that overhead
   Blue skies will brighten, and the sun
     will shine,
And flowers be sweet in many a garden
   bed,
     And all divine,
   (For are they not, O Father, thoughts
     of thine ?)
Earth's warmth and fragrance shall on
   men be shed.

And I am glad that Night will always
   come,
   Hushing all sounds, even the soft-voiced
     birds,
Putting away all light from her deep dome,
   Until are heard
   In the wide starlight's stillness, un-
     known words,

That make the heart ache till it find its
    home.

And I am glad that neither golden sky,
   Nor violet lights that linger on the hill,
Nor ocean's wistful blue shall satisfy,
     But they shall fill
  With wild unrest and endless longing
    still,
The soul whose hope beyond them all
    must lie.

And I rejoice that love shall never seem
   So perfect as it ever was to be,
But endlessly that inner haunting dream
     Each heart shall see
Hinted in every dawn's fresh purity,
Hopelessly shadowed in each sunset's
    gleam.

And though warm mouths will kiss and
    hands will cling,
  And thought by silent thought be under-
    stood,

I do rejoice that the next hour will bring
    That far off mood,
  That drives one like a lonely child to
    God,
Who only sees and measures everything.

And it is well that when these feet have
    pressed
The outward path from earth, 'twill not
    seem sad
To them that stay; but they who love me
    best
    Will be most glad
  That such a long unquiet now has had,
At last, a gift of perfect peace and rest.

THE SECRET

TIDE of sun and song in beauty
    broke
Against a bitter heart, where no
    voice woke
      Till thus it spoke : —

What was it, in the old time that I know,
That made the world with inner beauty
    glow,
      Now a vain show ?

Still dance the shadows on the grass at
    play,
Still move the clouds like great, calm
    thoughts away,
      Nor haste, nor stay.

But I have lost that breath within the
    gale,

That light to which the daylight was a veil,
The star-shine pale.

Still all the summer with its songs is
    filled,
But that delicious undertone they held —
    Why is it stilled ?

Then I took heart that I would find again
The voices that had long in silence lain,
    Nor live in vain.

I stood at noonday in the hollow wind,
Listened at midnight, straining heart and
    mind
    If I might find !

But all in vain I sought, at eve and morn,
On sunny seas, in dripping woods forlorn,
    Till tired and worn,

One day I left my solitary tent
And down into the world's bright garden
    went,
    On labor bent.

The dew stars and the buds about my feet
Began their old bright message to repeat,
    In odors sweet;

And as I worked at weed and root in
    glee,
Now humming and now whistling cheerily,
    It came to me, —

The secret of the glory that was fled
Shone like a sweep of sun all overhead,
    And something said, —

" The blessing came because it was not
    sought ;
There was no care if thou wert blest or
    not :
The beauty and the wonder all thy
    thought, —
    Thyself forgot."

LOST LOVE

URY it, and sift
　　Dust upon its light, —
Death must not be left,
　　To offend the sight.

Cover the old love —
　　Weep not on the mound —
Grass shall grow above,
　　Lilies spring around.

Can we fight the law,
　　Can our natures change —
Half-way through withdraw —
　　Other lives exchange?

You and I must do
　　As the world has done,
There is nothing new
　　Underneath the sun.

Fill the grave up full —
 Put the dead love by —
Not that men are dull,
 Not that women lie, —

But 't is well and right —
 Safest, you will find —
That the Out of Sight
 Should be Out of Mind.

APPRECIATED

"AH, could I but be understood!"
   (I prayed the powers above)
   "Could but some spirit, bright
       and good,
Know me and, knowing, love!"

One summer's day there came to pass —
   A maid; and it befell
She spied and knew me: yea, alas!
   She knew me all too well.

Gray were the eyes of Rosamund,
   And I could see them see
Through and through me, and beyond,
   And care no more for me.

AWN has blossomed: the sun is
    nigh :
Pearl and rose in the wimpled
    sky,
Rose and pearl on a brightening blue:
(She is true, and she is true !)

The noonday lies all warm and still
And calm, and over sleeping hill
And wheatfields falls a dreamy hue:
(If she be true — if she be true !)

The patient evening comes, most sad and
    fair :
Veiled are the stars : the dim and quiet air
Breathes bitter scents of hidden myrrh
    and rue :
(If she were true — if she were only
    true !)

LACK, frost-cold distance, sparse-
   ly honey-combed
   With hollow shells of glimmer-
     ing golden light ;
Mere amber bubbles floating through
   the night,
Lit by one centred sparkle, azure-domed,
With circling motes where life hath lodged
   and roamed.

UNTIMELY THOUGHT

LOOKED across the lawn one
summer's day,
Deep shadowed, dreaming in
the drowsy light,
And thought, what if this afternoon, so
bright
And still, should end it? — as it may.

Blue dome, and flocks of fleece that slowly
pass
Before the pale old moon, the while she
keeps
Her sleepy watch, and ancient pear that
sweeps
Its low, fruit-laden skirts along the grass.

What if I had to say to all of these,
"So this is the last time" — suddenly
there

My love came loitering under the great
  trees ;

And now the thought I could no longer
  bear :
Startled I flung it from me, as one flings
All sharply from the hand a bee that
  stings.

THE LIFE NATURAL

OVERHEAD the leaf-song, on the
    upland slope;
Over that the azure, clean from
    base to cope ;
Belle the mare beside me, drowsy from
    her lope.

Goldy-green the wheat-field, like a fluted
    wall
In the pleasant wind, with waves that rise
    and fall,
" Moving all together," if it " move at all."

Shakspere in my pocket, lest I feel alone,
Lest the brooding landscape take a som-
    bre tone ;
Good to have a poet to fall back upon !

But the vivid beauty makes the book
    absurd :

What beside the real world is the written
    word ?
Keep the page till winter, when no thrush
    is heard !

Why read Hamlet here ? — what 's Hecuba
    to me ?
Let me read the grain-field ; let me read
    the tree ;
Let me read mine own heart, deep as I
    can see.

THE ORACLE

DOWN in its crystal hollow
   Gleams the ebon well of ink:
In the deepest drop lies lurking
The thought all men shall think.

Fair on the waiting tablet
   Lies the empty paper's space:
Out of its snow shall flush a word
   Like an angel's earnest face.

Who in those depths shall cast his line
   For the gnome that hugs that thought?
Who from the snowy field shall charm
   That flower of truth untaught?

Not in the lore of the ancients,
   Not in the yesterday:
On the lips of the living moments
   The gods their message lay.

Somewhere near it is waiting,
   Like a night-wind wandering free,
Seeking a mouth to speak through, —
   Whose shall the message be?

It may steal forth like a flute note,
   It may be suddenly hurled
In blare upon blare of a trumpet blast,
   To startle and stir the world.

Hark! but just on the other side
   Some thinnest wall of dreams,
Murmurs a whispered music,
   And softest rose-light gleams.

Listen, and watch, and tell the world
   What it almost dies to know:
Or wait — and the wise old world will say,
   "I knew it long ago."

FORCE

THE stars know a secret
    They do not tell;
And morn brings a message
    Hidden well.

There's a blush on the apple,
    A tint on the wing,
And the bright wind whistles,
    And the pulses sting.

Perish dark memories!
    There's light ahead;
This world's for the living;
    Not for the dead.

In the shining city,
    On the loud pave,
The life-tide is running
    Like a leaping wave.

How the stream quickens,
　As noon draws near,
No room for loiterers,
　No time for fear.

Out on the farm lands
　Earth smiles as well;
Gold-crusted grain-fields,
　With sweet, warm smell;

Whir of the reaper,
　Like a giant bee;
Like a Titan cricket,
　Thrilling with glee.

On mart and meadow,
　Pavement or plain;
On azure mountain.
　Or azure main —

Heaven bends in blessing;
　Lost is but won;
Goes the good rain-cloud,
　Comes the good sun !

Only babes whimper,
   And sick men wail,
And faint hearts and feeble hearts,
   And weaklings fail.

Down the great currents
   Let the boat swing;
There was never winter
   But brought the spring.

SUNDOWN

SEA of splendor in the West,
    Purple, and pearl, and gold,
With milk-white ships of cloud,
    whose sails
Slowly the winds unfold.

Brown cirrus-bars, like ribbed beach-sand,
    Cross the blue upper dome ;
And nearer flecks of feathery white
    Blow over them like foam.

But when that transient glory dies
    Into the twilight gray,
And leaves me on the beach alone
    Beside the glimmering bay ;

And when I know that, late or soon,
    Love's glory finds a grave,
And hearts that danced like dancing foam
    Break like the breaking wave ;

70

A little dreary, homeless thought
   Creeps sadly over me,
Like the shadow of a lonely cloud
   Moving along the sea.

NIGHT AND PEACE

NIGHT in the woods, — night :
　　Peace, peace on the plain.
　The last red sunset beam
　Belts the tall beech with gold ;
　The quiet kine are in the fold,
And stilly flows the stream.
　　Soon shall we see the stars again,
　　For one more day down to its rest has
　　　　lain,
And all its cares have taken flight,
　And all its doubt and pain.
Night in the woods, — night :
　Peace, peace on the plain.

THE SINGER'S CONFESSION

NCE he cried to all the hills and
   waters
   And the tossing grain and tufted
   grasses :
"Take my message — tell it to my bro-
   thers !
Stricken mute I cannot speak my mes-
   sage.
When the evening wind comes back from
   ocean,
Singing surf-songs, to Earth's fragrant
   bosom,
And the beautiful young human creatures
Gather at the mother feet of Nature,
Gazing with their pure and wistful faces,
Tell the old heroic human story.
When they weary of the wheels of science,
Grinding, jangling their harsh disso-
   nances, —

Stones and bones and alkalis and
    atoms, —
Sing to them of human hope and passion;
And the soul divine, whose incarnation,
Born of love — alas! my message stum-
    bles,
Faints on faltering lips: Oh, speak it for
    me!"

Then a hush fell; and around about him
Suddenly he felt the mighty shadow
Of the hills, like grave and silent pity;
And, as one who sees without regarding,
The wide wind went over him and left
    him,
And the brook, repeating low, "His mes-
    sage!"
Babbled, as it fled, a quiet laughter.

What was he, that he had touched their
    message —
Theirs, who had been chanting it forever:
With whose organ-tones the human spirit
Had eternally been overflowing!

Then, with shame that stung in cheek and
       forehead,
Slow he crept away.
                   And now he listens,
Mute and still, to hear them tell their
       message —
All the holy hills and sacred waters ;
When the sea-wind swings its evening
       censer,
Till the misty incense hides the altar
And the long-robed shadows, lowly kneel-
       ing.

"TO-DAY," I thought, "I will not plan nor strive;
Idle as yon blue sky, or clouds that go
Like loitering ships, with sails as white as snow,
I simply will be glad to be alive."

For, year by year, in steady summer glow
The flowers had bloomed, and life had stored its hive,
But tasted not the honey. Quite to thrive,
The flavor of my thrift I now would know.

But the good breeze blew in a friend — a boon
At any hour. There was a book to show,
A gift to take, a slender one to give.

The morning passed to mellow afternoon,
And that to twilight; it was sleep-time
    soon, —
And lo! again I had forgot to live.

 TROOP of babes in Summer-
Land,
 At heaven's gate — the chil-
dren's gate :
One lifts the latch with rosy hand,
 Then turns and, dimpling, asks her
mate, —

"What was the last thing that you saw ?"
 "I lay and watched the dawn begin,
And suddenly, thro' the thatch of straw,
 A great, clear morning-star laughed in."

"And you ?" "A floating thistle-down,
 Against June sky and cloud - wings
white."
"And you ?" "A falling blow, a frown —
 It frights me yet ; oh, clasp me tight !"

"And you?" "A face thro' tears that
  smiled " —
  The trembling lips could speak no
    more ;
The blue eyes swam ; the lonely child
  Was homesick even at heaven's door.

 SAID: " Blue heaven " (Oh, it
    was beautiful !),
" Send me a tent to shut me to
    myself :
I am all lonely for my soul, that wanders
Weary, bewildered, beckoned by thy
    depths ;
Thy white, round clouds, great bubbles of
    creamy snow ;
Thy luscious sunshine, like some ripe, gold
    fruit ;
Thy songs of birds, and wind warm with
    the flowers."

And there swept down (Oh, it was beauti-
    ful !)
A tent of silver rain, that fell like a veil
Shutting me in to think all quiet thoughts,
And feel the vibrant thrill of shadowy
    wings

That fluttered, checking their swift flight,
    and hear,
Though with no syllable of earthly music,
A voice of melody unutterable.

 SEA of shade; with hollow
    heights above,
  Where floats the redwood's
    airy roof away,
Whose feathery lace the drowsy breezes
  move,
  And softly through the azure windows
    play :
  No nearer stir than yon white cloud
    astray,
No closer sound than sob of distant dove.

I only live as the deep forest's swoon
  Dreams me amid its dream ; for all
    things fade,
Nor pulse of mine disturbs the uncon-
  scious noon.
  Even love and hope are still — albeit
    they made

My heart beat yesterday — in slumber
 laid,
Like yon dim ghost that last night was
 the moon.

Only the bending grass, grown gray and
 sear,
 Nods now and then, where at my feet
 it swings,
Pleased that another like itself is here,
 Unseen among the mighty forest
 things —
Another fruitless life, that fading clings
To earth and autumn days in doubt and
 fear.

Dream on, O wood! O wind, stay in thy
 west,
 Nor wake the shadowy spirit of the
 fern,
Asleep along the fallen pine-tree's breast!
 That, till the sun go down, and night-
 stars burn,

And the chill dawn-breath from the sea
 return,
Tired earth may taste heaven's honey-dew
 of rest.

A MEMORY

UPON the barren, lonely hill
    We sat to watch the sinking
        sun;
Below, the land grew dim and still,
    Whose evening shadow had begun.
Her finger parted the shut book, —
    At Aylmer's Field the leaf was turned, —
Round her meek head and sainted look
    The sunset like a halo burned.
She knew not that I watched her face —
    Her spirit through her eyes was gone
To some far-off and Sabbath place,
    And left me gazing there alone.
Could she have known, that quiet hour,
    What ghosts her presence raised in me,
What graves were opened by the power
    Of that unconscious witchery,
She would not thus have sat and seen
    The bird that balanced far below

On the blue air, and watched the sheen
   Along his broad wings come and go.
For was she not another's bride?
   And I — what right had I to feast
Upon those eyes in revery wide,
   With hungering gaze like famished
      beast?
Was it before my fate I knelt —
   The human fate, the mighty law —
To hunger for the heart I felt,
   And love the lovely face I saw?
Or was it only that the brow,
   Or some sweet trick of hand or tone,
Brought from the Past to haunt me now
   Her ghost whose love was mine alone?
I know not; but we went to rest
   That eve, from songs that haunt me
      still,
And all night long, in visions blest,
   I walked with angels on the hill.

THE OPEN WINDOW

Y tower was grimly builded,
   With many a bolt and bar,
"And here," I thought, "I will
    keep my life
From the bitter world afar."

Dark and chill was the stony floor,
   Where never a sunbeam lay,
And the mould crept up on the dreary
    wall,
   With its ghost touch, day by day.

One morn, in my sullen musings,
   A flutter and cry I heard ;
And close at the rusty casement
   There clung a frightened bird.

Then back I flung the shutter
   That was never before undone,

And I kept till its wings were rested
  The little weary one.

But in through the open window,
  Which I had forgot to close,
There had burst a gush of sunshine
  And a summer scent of rose.

For all the while I had burrowed
  There in my dingy tower,
Lo ! the birds had sung and the leaves
    had danced
  From hour to sunny hour.

And such balm and warmth and beauty
  Came drifting in since then,
That the window still stands open
  And shall never be shut again.

ON A PICTURE OF MT. SHASTA
BY KEITH

TWO craggy slopes, sheer down on
    either hand,
  Fall to a cleft, dark and confused
    with pines.
Out of their sombre shade — one gleam
    of light —
Escaping toward us like a hurrying child,
Half laughing, half afraid, a white brook
    runs.
The fancy tracks it back thro' the thick
    gloom
Of crowded trees, immense, mysterious
As monoliths of some colossal temple,
Dusky with incense, chill with endless
    time:
Thro' their dim arches chants the distant
    wind,
Hollow and vast, and ancient oracles
Whisper, and wait to be interpreted.

Far up the gorge denser and darker grows
The forest; columns lie with writhen roots
      in air,
And across open glades the sunbeams
      slant
To touch the vanishing wing-tips of shy
      birds;
Till from a mist-rolled valley soar the
      slopes,
Blue-hazy, dense with pines to the verge
      of snow,
Up into cloud. Suddenly parts the cloud,
And lo! in heaven — as pure as very
      snow,
Uplifted like a solitary world —
A star, grown all at once distinct and
      clear —
The white earth-spirit, Shasta! Calm,
      alone,
Silent it stands, cold in the crystal air,
White - bosomed sister of the stainless
      dawn,
With whom the cloud holds converse, and
      the storm

Rests there, and stills its tempest into
    snow.

Once — you remember ? — we beheld that
    vision,
But busy days recalled us, and the whole
Fades now among my memories like a
    dream.
The distant thing is all incredible,
And the dim past as if it had not been.
Our world flees from us ; only the one
    point,
The unsubstantial moment, is our own.
We are but as the dead, save that swift
    mote
Of conscious life.   Then the great artist
    comes,
Commands the chariot wheels of Time to
    stay,
Summons the distant, as by some austere
Grand gesture of a mighty sorcerer's wand,
And our whole world again becomes our
    own.
So we escape the petty tyranny

Of the incessant hour; pure thought
    evades
Its customary bondage, and the mind
Is lifted up, watching the moon-like globe.

How should a man be eager or perturbed
Within this calm?   How should he greatly
    care
For reparation, or redress of wrong, —
To scotch the liar, or spurn the fawning
    knave,
Or heed the babble of the ignoble crew?
Seest thou yon blur far up the icy slope,
Like a man's footprint?   Half thy little
    town
Might hide there, or be buried in what
    seems
From yonder cliff a curl of feathery snow.
Still the far peak would keep its frozen
    calm,
Still at the evening on its pinnacle
Would the one tender touch of sunset
    dwell,
And o'er it nightlong wheel the silent stars.

So the great globe rounds on, — moun-
    tains, and vales,
Forests, waste stretches of gaunt rock and
    sand,
Shore, and the swaying ocean, — league
    on league ;
And blossoms open, and are sealed in
    frost ;
And babes are born, and men are laid to
    rest.
What is this breathing atom, that his
    brain
Should build or purpose aught or aught
    desire,
But stand a moment in amaze and awe,
Rapt on the wonderfulness of the world ?

THE TREE OF MY LIFE

HEN I was yet but a child, the
gardener gave me a tree,
A little slim elm, to be set wher-
ever seemed good to me.

What a wonderful thing it seemed! with
its lace-edge leaves uncurled,
And its span-long stem, that should grow
to the grandest tree in the world.

So I searched all the garden round, and
out over field and hill,
But not a spot could I find that suited my
wayward will.

I would have it bowered in the grove, in a
close and quiet vale ;
I would rear it aloft on the height, to
wrestle with the gale.

Then I said, " I will cover its roots with
a little earth by the door,

And there it shall live and wait, while I
    search for a place once more.
But still I could never find it, the place
    for my wondrous tree,
And it waited and grew by the door, while
    years passed over me.
Till suddenly, one fine day, I saw it was
    grown too tall,
And its roots gone down too deep, to be
    ever moved at all.

So here it is growing still, by the lowly
    cottage door ;
Never so grand and tall as I dreamed it
    would be of yore,
But it shelters a tired old man in its sun-
    shine-dappled shade,
The children's pattering feet round its
    knotty knees have played,
Dear singing birds in a storm sometimes
    take refuge there,
And the stars through its silent boughs
    shine gloriously fair.

A CHILD AND A STAR

HE star, so pure in saintly white,
Deep in the solemn soul of night,
With dreams of deathless beauty
    wed,
And golden ways that seraphs tread :
The child — so mere a thing of earth,
So meek a flower of mortal birth :
A far-off lucent world, so bright,
Stooping to touch with tender light
That little gown at evening prayer :
It seems a condescension rare, —
Heaven round a common child to glow !
Ah ! wiser eyes of angels know
The star, a toy but roughly wrought ;
The child, God's own most loving thought.
Yon evening planet, wan with moons,
Colossal, 'mid its dim, swift noons, —
What is it but a bulk of stone,
Like this gray globe we dwell upon ?

Down hollow spaces, sightless, chill,
Its vibrant beams in darkness thrill,
Till thro' some window drift the rays
Where a pure heart looks up and prays;
And in that silent worshipper,
The waves of feeling stir and stir,
And spread in wider rings above,
To tremble at God's heart of love.
Tho' it be kingliest one of all
His worlds, 't is but a stony ball:
What are they all, from sun to sun,
But dust and stubble, when all 's done?
Some heavenly grace it only caught,
When, like a hint from home, it brought
To a child's heart one tender thought:
Itself in that great mystery lost,
As some bright pebble, idly tost
Into the darkling sea at night,
Whose widening ripples, running light,
Go out into the infinite.

 LAY awake and listened, ere the light

Began to whiten at the window pane.

The world was all asleep: earth was a fane

Emptied of worshippers; its dome of night,

Its silent aisles, were awful in their gloom.

Suddenly from the tower the bell struck four,

Solemn and slow, how slow and solemn! o'er

Those death-like slumberers, each within his room.

The last reverberation pulsed so long

It seemed no tone of earthly mould at all.

But the bell woke a thrush; and with a call

He roused his mate, then poured a tide of song :

" Morning is coming, fresh, and clear, and
    blue,"
Said that bright song ; and then I thought
    of you.

AN ADAGE FROM THE ORIENT

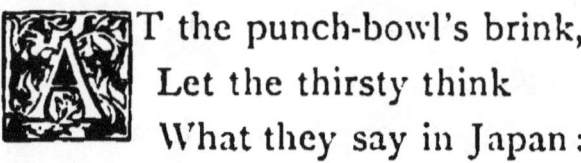T the punch-bowl's brink,
Let the thirsty think
What they say in Japan:

" First the man takes a drink,
Then the drink takes a drink,
Then the drink takes the man!"

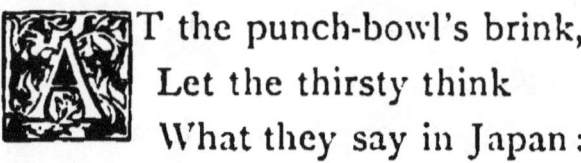

100

A PARADOX

HASTE, haste, O laggard! — leave
thy drowsy dreams;
Cram all thy brain with know-
ledge — clutch and cram!
The earth is wide, the universe is vast:
Thou hast infinity to learn. Oh, haste!

Haste not, haste not, my soul! "Infin-
ity!"
Thou hast eternity to learn it in.
Thy boundless lesson through the endless
years
Hath boundless leisure. Run not like a
slave —
Sit like a king, and see the ranks of worlds
Wheel in their cycles onward to thy feet.

THE PHILOSOPHER

HIS wheel of logic whirled and
    spun all day ;
   All day he held his system,
    grinding it
Finer and finer, till 't was fined away.

  But the chance sparks of sense and
    mother-wit,
Flung out as that wheel-logic spun and
    whirled,
Kindled the nations, and lit up the world.

A BIRD'S SONG

HE shadow of a bird
  On the shadow of a bough ;
Sweet and clear his song is
  heard,
" Seek me now — I seek thee now."
The bird swings out of reach in the sway-
  ing tree,
But his shadow on the garden walk below
  belongs to me.

The phantom of my Love
  False dreams with hope doth fill,
Softly singing far above,
  " Love me still — I love thee still ! "
The cruel vision hovers at my sad heart's
  door,
But the soul love is soaring out of reach
  for evermore.

THE DEAD PRESIDENT

ERE there no crowns on earth,
　　No evergreen to weave a hero's
　　　　wreath,
That he must pass beyond the gates of
　　death,
Our hero, our slain hero, to be crowned?
Could there on our unworthy earth be
　　found
　　Naught to befit his worth?

　　The noblest soul of all!
When was there ever, since our Washing-
　　ton,
A man so pure, so wise, so patient —
　　one
Who walked with this high goal alone in
　　sight,
To speak, to do, to sanction only Right,
　　Though very heaven should fall!

Ah, not for him we weep;
What honor more could be in store for
    him ?
Who would have had him linger in our
    dim
And troublesome world, when his great
    work was done —
Who would not leave that worn and weary
    one
    Gladly to go to sleep?

For us the stroke was just ;
We were not worthy of that patient heart ;
We might have helped him more, not
    stood apart,
And coldly criticised his works and
    ways —
Too late now, all too late — our little
    praise
    Sounds hollow o'er his dust.

Be merciful, O our God !
Forgive the meanness of our human
    hearts,

That never, till a noble soul departs,
See half the worth, or hear the angel's
    wings
Till they go rustling heavenward as he
    springs
  Up from the mounded sod.

  Yet what a deathless crown
Of Northern pine and Southern orange-
    flower,
For victory, and the land's new bridal-
    hour,
Would we have wreathed for that beloved
    brow!
Sadly upon his sleeping forehead now
  We lay our cypress down.

  O martyred one, farewell!
Thou hast not left thy people quite alone,
Out of thy beautiful life there comes a
    tone
Of power, of love, of trust, a prophecy,
Whose fair fulfillment all the earth shall be,
  And all the Future tell.

A FOOLISH creature full of fears,
  He trembled for his fate,
And stood aghast to feel the earth
Swing round her dizzy freight.

With timid foot he touched each plan,
  Sure that each plan would fail;
Behemoth's tread was his, it seemed,
  And every bridge too frail.

No glory of the night or day
  Lit any crown for him,
The tranquil past but breathed a mist
  To make the future dim.

The world, his birthright, seemed a cell,
  An iron heritage;
Man, a trapped creature, left to die
  Forgotten in his cage.

In every dark he held his breath,
   And warded off a blow;
While at his shoulder still he sought
   Some tagging ghost of woe.

Spying the thorns but not the flowers,
   Through all the blossoming land
He hugged his careful heart and shunned
   The path on either hand.

The buds that broke their hearts to give
   New odors to the air
He saw not; but he caught the scent
   Of dead leaves everywhere.

Till on a day he came to know
   He had not made the world;
That if he slept, as when he ran,
   Each onward planet whirled.

He knew not where the vision fell,
   Only all things grew plain —
As if some thatch broke through and let
   A sunbeam cross his brain.

In beauty flushed the morning light,
  With blessing dropped the rain,
All creatures were to him most fair,
  Nor anything in vain.

He breathed the space that links the stars,
  He rested on God's arm —
A man unmoved by accident,
  Untouched by any harm.

The weary doubt if all is good,
  The doubt if all is ill,
He left to Him who leaves to us
  To know that all is well.